DISNEY MOANA

Adapted by
Laura Hitchcock

Illustrated by
Griselda Sastrawinata-Lemay

Designed by
Tony Fejeran

*A special thanks to the wonderful people of the Pacific Islands for inspiring
us on this journey as we bring the world of Moana to life.*

A GOLDEN BOOK · NEW YORK

randomhousekids.com

ISBN 978-0-7364-3603-8 (trade) — ISBN 978-0-7364-3604-5 (ebook)

Printed in the United States of America

10 9

Even when she was little,
Moana of Motunui
LOVED
the ocean.

She also loved listening to Gramma Tala's stories. Moana's favorite was about the trickster **demigod Maui,** who stole the heart of the mother island, Te Fiti.

According to Gramma, Maui upset the **balance of nature** by stealing the heart.

Moana's dad, Chief Tui, believed the ocean was dangerous. The islanders were forbidden to sail beyond the reef!

But little Moana felt a deep connection to the ocean, and to all the creatures who belonged in it. She always wanted to help.

And the ocean noticed! It gave Moana a

special gift.

When Chief Tui
picked up Moana, she
dropped the gift.

Luckily, someone
else picked it up.

It was Gramma Tala!
She believed the ocean's
gift was the heart of

Te Fiti!

As she grew, Moana worked hard to help lead her people and follow her father's rules. But when Moana turned sixteen, Gramma Tala took her aside. "It's time to learn who you were meant to be," Gramma said. She led Moana to a hidden cavern . . .

. . . full of **ancient canoes.**

When Moana started drumming,

Bam!

Bam!

Bam!

she could feel the spirits of her ancestors.
They were **wayfinders**—voyagers on
the ocean!

Gramma Tala's last wish was for Moana to journey across the ocean, find Maui, and restore the heart of Te Fiti.

So, with the heart safe inside her necklace, **Moana set sail.**

But sailing on the open ocean was not easy
for Moana—especially when a **storm** hit!

Moana and her boat washed up on
a faraway island, where she met

Maui
the demigod!

He was NOT what Moana expected.

Maui stole Moana's boat!
But when he tried to sail away, the ocean
made sure Moana went with him.

The ocean wanted them to work together.

Along the way, Maui taught Moana how to wayfind, which is to use the **sun,** the **stars,**

the **moon,**

and the **ocean current** to navigate.

And when the journey became too difficult, the spirit of Gramma Tala returned. "Know who you are meant to be," Gramma's spirit told Moana.

When Moana and Maui finally reached
Te Fiti, the mother island was gone. Instead,
there was a **lava monster** named

Te Kā!

Maui and Moana tried
everything, but they could
not defeat Te Kā.

Then Moana
had an idea.